EASY STREET

EASY STREET

Jeff Ross

orca soundings

ORCA BOOK PUBLISHERS

Library and Archives Canada Cataloguing in Publication

Title: Easy street / Jeff Ross.
Names: Ross, Jeff, 1973– author.
Series: Orca soundings.
Description: Series statement: Orca soundings

Identifiers: Canadiana (print) 20190168374 | Canadiana (ebook) 20190168587 |
ISBN 9781459824010 (softcover) | ISBN 9781459824027 (PDF) |
ISBN 9781459824034 (EPUB)

Classification: LCC PS8635.06928 E27 2020 | DDC jc813/.6—dc23

Library of Congress Control Number: 2019944498
Simultaneously published in Canada and the United States in 2020

Summary: In this high-interest novel for teen readers, Rob has
mixed feelings about his brother, Adam, being released from prison.

*Orca Book Publishers is committed to reducing the consumption
of nonrenewable resources in the making of our books. We make
every effort to use materials that support a sustainable future.*

Orca Book Publishers gratefully acknowledges the support for its
publishing programs provided by the following agencies: the Government
of Canada, the Canada Council for the Arts and the Province of British
Columbia through the BC Arts Council and the Book Publishing Tax Credit.

Edited by Tanya Trafford
Cover images by Gettyimages.ca/Tanzim Mokammel/EyeEm (front) and
Shutterstock.com/Krasovski Dmitri (back)

ORCA BOOK PUBLISHERS
orcabook.com

Printed and bound in Canada.

23 22 21 20 • 4 3 2 1

To Ros and Bill

Chapter One

There was a delay in Adam's release. We were told this is common. Not by the guards or officials at the prison, but by a woman there to collect her husband.

"He's been up in here before," she said. "But this is the last time. As far as I'm concerned anyhow. He gets himself put up in here again, he'll get out to find no one waiting."

My mom smiled at her and carried on a brief, stilted conversation before the woman recognized someone and changed seats.

After that we sat in silence in the little waiting room. It wasn't like the movies. Big doors did not slowly open. No one was slipping into a fast car and tearing off toward freedom. Mom and I had arrived in our red VW Golf, the same car we'd had since Adam and I were kids. We'd filled out a bunch of paperwork, then been told to wait. People came and went. At one point a van pulled up outside, and six men in orange jumpsuits, all cuffed together, were paraded through the waiting area and into the darkness of the prison.

"This place..." Mom began, then lowered her voice as though someone might be offended. "This place is horrible."

When Adam finally arrived it was without any fanfare. He was led to the reception desk and uncuffed. A guard dropped a sheet of paper and a pen in front of him. Adam signed wherever the guard placed his finger.

"Releasing prisoner!" the guard yelled, handing Adam a see-through bag of clothing.

"Prisoner released!" a guard called back.

And that was it. Adam walked past the desk and into the dim light of the waiting room.

Mom looked like she wanted to hug him, but other men were being released at the same time. Big men whose eyes already seemed to be searching for the next hustle in this new world of freedom. Adam didn't look like he wanted to be hugged anyway.

"Hey," Adam said. He was thinner

but bigger at the same time. I guess leaner.

"Oh, Adam," Mom said. She looked like she might cry, so we turned her around, and the three of us walked out of there into the blue glow of early evening.

"What took so long?" Mom asked when we were in the car. I'd slipped into the back seat, and before I knew what was happening, Adam had as well.

"I don't know. They don't tell you much in there," Adam replied.

"Isn't someone going to ride up here with me?" It was an hour-and-a-half drive from the prison to our house.

"I'm good," Adam said. He pulled his hoodie out of the clear bag and pushed it against the window. Then he rested his head on it.

"I guess I will," I said. I jumped out of the car and got into the front passenger seat.

No one said anything for a while. Then we were on the highway, and evening was changing to night.

"So what are your plans?" Mom asked.

"I don't know," Adam replied.

I glanced back. He was staring out the window. I remembered all the trips we'd taken before. Adam could always fall asleep in the car, but I never could. I was always too jumpy. I wanted to see everything and was freaked out that something was going to happen and I would miss it. Adam could sleep anywhere. Anytime.

"You're going to need some," said Mom. "Plans, that is. You're not just coming back home to do nothing." I could see her hands tightening on the steering wheel. She'd talked a lot about how things were going to be different. How she needed to be around more to help steer her boys. She'd tried dating a little, but all the guys had seemed uninterested in us and were gone before they could plant any kind of roots. It had felt like it was just the two of us against the world over the past couple of years.

Now we were three again.

"Uh-huh," Adam grunted.

"I got you an appointment with your career counselor tomorrow," said Mom. Adam didn't respond. "He sees a couple of options for you right now. One, you finish off high school, which is something that's going to happen one way or another, and then find a job. He recommends considering the trades. Lots of demand for those. Or you could look into fast-tracking by joining an apprenticeship program. That way you'd be able to learn on the job and finish up your high school at night. The bonus is that you'd likely have a job waiting for you when you finish. Anyway, you see him tomorrow at ten. I can't be there with you because I have to work. He seems pretty positive about your possibilities. It's not going to be easy. Some people look at people like you who have been where you've been and they can't get past it. They think, *A leopard never changes his spots*, right? But I don't see it that way. I don't see it that way at all. I think you did what you did, you paid for it, and now you're back out. Clean slate. That's the way I see it." She paused and wiped at her cheek with the back of her hand. "How do *you* see it, Adam?"

I looked back at my brother. The lights of oncoming cars rode across him. I wondered what he'd seen inside. I wondered if he regretted what he'd done. He had to regret it, right? He had to have learned something.

But most of all I wondered if I could ever forgive him.

"Adam?" Mom said again, rising up in her seat and tilting the rearview mirror to look into the back seat.

"I think he's asleep," I said.

"What?" She wiped at her cheek with the back of her hand again.

"I think he's asleep." She returned the mirror to its original position and wrapped her hands around the steering wheel.

"What are we going to do with him, Rob?" she said. I wanted to tell her that it was going to be okay. That things would work out. That he had learned something in prison and wouldn't go off the rails again. But I had no idea if that was true. I had no idea who my brother had become.

Chapter Two

Over the next few days Adam visited his career counselor, his employment counselor, his Narcotics Anonymous sponsor (because even though he never touched drugs himself, assumptions were made due to the nature of his crime) and, finally, his parole officer.

I went with him to that meeting. His parole officer was a big man named Steve.

He had a perfectly shaved head, and each of his giant fingers sported at least one flashy ring. Whenever he rotated his hands, the rings caught the sun streaming through the diner's window. When we walked in Steve was at a table, twirling a spoon in a cup. As we sat down across from him, I noticed that there wasn't any milk in his coffee. He kept twirling the spoon for almost a minute more.

"Stirring oxygenates the coffee," he said, looking up at us. He took a sip, smiled and then set the mug back down on the table. "You caught me at the right time, Adam." He took another sip. "Half an hour earlier I would have been one grumpy man. You guys drink coffee?"

I shook my head, even though coffee had become a morning necessity.

"Sure," Adam said.

Steve put up an arm, and the server came over. "Cup of coffee for my friend," Steve said.

"Anything to eat?" she asked.

"How about a plate of toast?"

The server patted him on the shoulder and walked away.

"I was just looking over your file, Adam," Steve said. "First offense, I see. I always like to know, when someone is listed as a first offender, was it the first time they did anything wrong? Or just the first time they got caught?"

I glanced over at Adam. My brother was giving Steve a hard stare. One I'd never seen before.

"It was a misunderstanding," Adam said.

Steve raised an eyebrow and turned the page of the file in front of him. "A misunderstanding where a girl ended up dead." He poked a finger on the page and then looked back up. "That's one hell of a misunderstanding."

The server returned and set a plate of toast on the table, pulled a selection of jams from her apron pocket and sprinkled them around the plate. She had apparently forgotten Adam's coffee, but he didn't say anything.

"Need to be somewhere?" Steve asked. Adam didn't respond. "You seem a bit edgy."

"I'm good," Adam said.

Steve glanced at me, then back at the file. "So what's your plan, Adam?" He took a piece of bread so well buttered that it was limp. He poked at the little packages of jam, selected one, tore it open and squeezed it onto the top of the bread.

"I don't know yet," Adam replied.

"That's what I thought you'd say. Have you hooked up with your employment counselor?"

"Yeah."

"What she got for you?"

"Probably nothing," Adam said.

"We got all kinds of programs, you know. Did she explain that to you?"

Adam sat back in the seat and crossed his arms. "She talked a lot about jobs with a whole bunch of other ex-cons."

"What's wrong with that?"

"Like I said, what happened to me was a misunderstanding. I never should've been inside."

Steve nodded a few times, then took a couple of giant bites from his toast. He brushed crumbs from the file and turned another page. "It says here you showed remorse for your crime." He looked up, his big eyes staring at Adam. "But now you're sitting here telling me it was all a misunderstanding." He leaned back in his seat. It creaked. "That doesn't sound very remorseful. It sounds more resentful."

"I'm sorry she died," Adam said. "I'm just saying it wasn't my fault."

"Oh, not your fault?" Steve said. He took another bite of toast, nodding as he chewed. "Then why do you suppose you went to jail?"

"Because I was stupid," Adam said.

"Explain."

"I never should have gotten involved. I never should have been in the middle. I never should have given her that pill."

Steve nodded a few times, then selected another jam, ripped it open and started smearing it on a new piece of toast.

"Sounds like remorse to me."

Adam shrugged. "So how often do we meet?"

"They say once a week. But I like to go with the flow. How often do you think we should meet?"

"Depends on why we're meeting," Adam said.

"You know, shoot the shit, hang out, eat some toast."

"That all?"

"I also have to make certain you're still living in your mother's house.

That you're not part of some criminal organization. That you're keeping yourself clean both in body and in mind. That kind of stuff. So the question is, how long can I have you out there running around before I need to check in and make sure everything's cool?" Steve stared at Adam as he chewed.

Adam cracked his little half smile, the first time I'd seen it since he returned. He liked these kinds of games. This verbal sparring.

"Twice a year sounds good," Adam said.

"That would get me fired and you tossed back in jail. Why don't we start off with every two weeks and see how that goes?"

Adam shrugged. "We good?" He slid out of the booth and stood up.

Steve nodded. "We're good, Adam. For now. But you need to stay good."

"Two weeks," Adam said.

"Anything changes, you need to call or text me." He handed Adam a card. Adam put it into his pocket, then headed for the door without another word.

I slipped out of the booth and followed him, feeling Steve's eyes on me as I went. I stepped in beside Adam as he made his way down the sidewalk. It was an impossibly blue sky. No clouds. Just clear and light blue, like the ocean turned upside down.

"That was weird," I said.

Adam was wearing his leather jacket even though it was warm out. "It's not weird, Rob," he said. "That's my life now. It's like I've got a hundred mothers. Everyone telling me what I can and can't do. What I should or shouldn't do. Where I can or can't be."

I hadn't spent any time with Adam during that first week. He'd just gone to appointments, come home and disappeared into his room. Mom had said the night before that it was like living with a stranger. I had to agree.

"So what are you going to do?" I asked.

Adam froze. He looked off across the street. "Don't you have things to do? Friends to go hang with or something?"

"Sure," I said. Although I didn't. I could see my question really bugged him.

"Maybe you should then. I need some time to think. So that the *next time* someone asks me what I'm going to do, maybe I'll have an answer."

"Okay," I said. "See you at home?"

"Yeah," Adam said as he stepped into the street. "See you at home."

Chapter Three

Mom and I were on the front porch when Adam came home the next day. He'd been home the previous night but had left before either of us was out of bed. Mom and I were catching the end-of-the-day sunshine that hits our porch. It had been a long winter. Now that summer was around the corner, I was finally feeling alive again.

Adam had a big smile on his face. He was in his leather jacket again, his jeans slightly too big for his frame. We were reflected in his sunglasses.

"I'm going back to college," he said.

I felt Mom tense beside me.

"That's great," she said. Before Adam was released, she and I had been given some training on how to behave. What to expect. One of the suggestions was that we be encouraging as long as whatever Adam was interested in was healthy. "What are you thinking of taking?"

Adam spun around and sat beside Mom. I felt something flow through me then. Except for the gap when Adam was in prison, it had been like this since Dad left. The three of us against the world. But when Adam went to prison, everything changed. It had been just Mom and I bumping into each other in the house. It wasn't as though we didn't talk or anything. We hung out, had a lot of meals together. But I wasn't a problem. I did what I had to do at school. I was planning for the future. I was getting good grades, and after graduation the world would be mine for the taking.

Adam had always been a problem. Like Dad. The two of them couldn't have been more alike. Mom and I had worried about Adam being in prison. We had no idea what kinds of things happened in there. We constantly wondered if he was all right, although there was nothing we could do about it. Eventually we got used to the feeling.

"I'm not sure yet. I'm interested in Humber, I think."

"In Toronto."

"Yeah. I mean, I don't know. I looked at their website today, and there's all kinds of stuff I'd like to try. I just don't know what I'd be best at."

"What kind of programs are you thinking of?"

"Some of the arts ones seem cool. There's a fitness one as well. I got into weights and training in...well, in the past year or so."

"Okay," Mom said. I could tell she was already wondering where the money would come from.

"If you're worried about money, there are some grants I can get. And loans. All that."

"I'm more concerned with the fact that you haven't graduated from high school yet."

"Well, they have this program there where I can finish high school first, take a couple of courses to get an idea of what it's all like, and then apply for the next year."

"You're thinking of going this September?" Mom asked. I wouldn't say she sounded that encouraging.

Adam stood again. He seemed really hyper.

"I've wasted enough time," he said. "I want to *do* something."

I could understand this. He'd spent the past two and a half years sitting around. Waiting.

"Well, let's look online and see—"

"I want to go down there and actually see the campus."

"When?"

"As soon as possible," Adam said. "The courses I can take to finish high school run all the time. I could start in the summer and then take some courses in the fall in whatever program I decide to go into. Graphic design looks interesting."

Adam seemed like his old self again. The one prior to his stint as a middleman for drug dealers. The one before he got lost in high school and couldn't find anything that interested him. The Adam who'd once been my best friend and brother.

Still, I had a bad feeling about it.

"Can we borrow the car tomorrow? Go to Toronto and see what's what?"

"We?" Mom asked.

"Rob and I."

I sat up. "You want me to go with you?"

"Yeah, why not? We can talk. And I'd like your opinion on the place. You know?"

I looked at Mom. I could tell she was trying to read him too. Which Adam did we have in front of us? The sweet kid who'd always looked for our approval? Or the one who had lied and plotted to get whatever he wanted?

I imagine we were both hoping it was the first one but frightened it was the second.

"What do you think, Rob?" Adam asked.

I hadn't traveled at all since we'd followed Adam here. It had seemed as though exploring the world was for other people. The ones who had fewer worries. Maybe a future me would be able to do that.

Despite all of this running through my head, I said, "That could be cool."

"You want to go tomorrow?" Mom said.

"First thing," Adam replied.

"I guess so," said Mom. "I can take the bus to work."

Adam leaned down and threw his arms around her neck. "Thanks, Mom. I am pumped about this." He let her go and went inside.

I caught Mom wiping her cheek with the back of her hand again.

"You think he's for real?" she asked without looking at me.

"I'll be there," I said. "I'll look out for him."

She nodded. "I know you will." She patted my knee and inhaled deeply.

"You're a good brother. A good son."
She squeezed my knee. "You're a good
person, Rob. So is Adam. He just needs
a little help sometimes to remember
that."

"Or believe it," I said. But I don't
think she heard me.

Chapter Four

The sun was just beginning to creep over the horizon as we pulled out of the driveway the next morning. Adam had tossed me the keys before getting in on the passenger side. He seemed very alert. He'd always been a night owl, but I figured prison had changed that.

"Let's hit Timmy's on the way out," he said, setting his seat almost straight up.

This was new as well. He used to sit low in a car, the brim of his hat just above the steering wheel. I pulled into the Tim Hortons at the southern end of town. We went inside to order. When it came time to pay, he looked to me. Luckily, Mom had given me some money.

"I'll get the next one," Adam said. The deep aroma of black coffee filled the car as we pulled back onto the road. I ate my breakfast sandwich and tried to relax. Not easy. It had been so long since I'd spent this kind of time with my brother that it was awkward to start a conversation. Anything to do with prison was out of bounds. Anything to do with Mary Jane's death or what had happened to us all as a family over the past two and a half years.

It seemed as though Adam wanted to pretend nothing had happened. Like it had all been a bad dream, gone now that we were awake.

It was a four-hour drive to Toronto. Almost a straight shot south. At first Adam had the heat cranked, but an hour into the trip he turned it off and cracked the rear windows to let in some fresh air.

"That's cool that you're interested in graphic design," I said. We'd been silent for a long time, and it was becoming unbearable.

"Remember when we used to go to that cottage in Muskoka?" he replied, completely ignoring my prompt.

"Barry and Carol's?"

"Yeah, that was them," Adam said, snapping his fingers. "Dad's friends, right?"

"I guess. We kept going once Dad was gone."

"Yeah. But I think I remember that Barry and Carol weren't there when we went just with Mom. It was, like, we went from being invited up in the middle of August when it was hot to either June or September. We weren't prime time anymore."

"I guess," I said. I couldn't remember the dates. It was a cottage we got to go to. There was a lake we swam in. Boats we rowed around. The bugs weren't bad either. Thinking back, I also remembered necessary campfires and heavy blankets.

"Good times," he said.

"In school I took a photography and graphic-design class," I said, hoping to get him tell me more.

"How was that?"

"Better than math or French."

"I bet."

"I can see why you're interested in it. Have you, like, been doing that kind of stuff the past couple of years?"

Adam glanced over at me, then tuned the radio to a different station. "Not a lot of cameras or computers in there," he said finally.

"Oh." Now I felt stupid for bringing it up.

"There was one computer in the library, but we only got to go there a couple of times a week. And it wasn't like they had Photoshop on it or anything."

"So have you been reading design magazines? There are tons of them."

"Yeah," Adam said.

"Which ones?" I wanted to tell him that I was interested in graphic design as well. DJing used to be my creative output. When I quit performing, I needed something else to feed my imagination. I started taking photos and mashing them up. Just like I used to do with beats and songs. I wouldn't say my stuff was any good, but it was passable. Better than what a lot of kids in my class spewed out anyway.

"I forget."

"Okay," I said, deciding to let it drop. "Did you set up appointments to see anyone on campus while we're down there?"

"It's Friday."

"There'll be people there on Friday."

"I just want to get a feel for everything first."

"I get it. Find some program information and all that. See what the place is like, right?"

"Yeah."

"Cool."

We drove in silence for a bit. Then my brother asked a question that surprised me. "You think Mom wants to stay up there?"

I decided honestly was the best way to answer. "We only moved for you," I said. Adam nodded a few times, and I wondered if that sounded awful. Like, we'd moved to what was obviously a crappy place in order to be close to him. The thing was, where we'd lived before was no dream either.

"Yeah. I was just thinking. Maybe Toronto would be better for her now. More work? Higher pay?"

"We were kind of waiting for you to come back before we made any big decisions."

"Well," he said, "I'm back." He set his seat back slightly and rolled his window down a crack.

We got into the city just after one o'clock and immediately hit traffic. I'd had my phone GPS set to Humber College's lakefront campus, but as soon as we crossed the 401, Adam started giving me directions.

"First we hit the Don Valley Parkway, then Richmond, Sherbourne, Queen."

"Where are we going?"

"Just drive, okay?"

I hate driving in the city. There are always pedestrians coming out of nowhere, bike couriers, other cars. It is pure chaos. As soon as we got onto

Queen Street, I started wishing I'd stayed home.

"Seriously, Adam. Where are we going?"

"I'm meeting up with a friend," he said. "Don't worry—we'll get to the college eventually."

I did worry. I worried a lot. "Take George Street here," Adam said. I turned, and Adam pulled a little piece of paper from his pocket. "Pull in here."

"Where?"

"Right here. The alleyway."

I did as I was told. He was my brother, after all. Even if I knew better, I Still Trusted Him.

Chapter Five

The basement apartment was incredibly hot. The guy who let us in was wearing a dirt-covered sleeveless T-shirt and cut-off jeans. He removed his glasses and wiped his face with a handkerchief.

"Adam?" he said.

"Yeah."

"This your brother?"

"Yeah. Rob."

"You spin mad beats?" the guy asked me.

I stared blankly. Adam pulled another piece of paper from his pocket and handed it to the guy. I recognized it as one of my old flyers.

"DJ Rob Solo. *Star Wars* nerd, are you?" he asked me.

I turned to Adam, but he was avoiding making eye contact. What was going on? He'd said we had a stop to make, that was all.

"Whatever," the guy continued. "If you can spin that old techno stuff, that's all that matters."

There was music playing. I hadn't noticed it before. I instantly knew the song. I guess my face must have given me away, because the guy said, "Yeah? Yeah? What is it?"

"Photek," I said. *"The Hidden Camera."*

The guy nodded a couple of times, then shut the door behind us. "Those were the days. Hard beats. Only a few people even making this stuff. So you had to be good. Not all this remixing and auto-tune and guest vocalists. This," he said, snapping his head to the beat. "*This* was music. Anyway, come on in here. We can talk while I finish what I was doing."

We walked through the kitchen. The temperature rose as we crossed the room. When the guy opened the door on the other side, we were hit by a wave of tropical heat. It felt warmer than the warmest summer day. But also wet and muggy.

"I'm Ben, by the way."

"I figured," Adam said.

"Mike says you can help us."

"We can," Adam said.

Ben's glasses had steamed up. He removed them and wiped the lenses with his handkerchief. The room was a serious grow op. Pot plants were stacked on three levels, plastic covering everything to keep in the heat and moisture. I had never been anywhere so bright before. "Your brother cool with his part?"

"That's the bit I don't understand yet," Adam said.

Ben replaced his glasses and wiped at his head. "Yeah, okay," he said. He went to a computer and removed a plastic wrap from it. "We had this guy lined up for the DJ part. DJ Oaklay. Like the sunglasses but with an *a*. Anyway, he got busted last week for something. I don't know what, and I don't much care. All I know is he's now unavailable. So we need another DJ. Honestly, the DJ isn't even in on this. He's just our way in." Ben turned to me, removed his glasses again, wiped them dry, then replaced them.

He looked at Adam. "Does he know what's going on?"

"No," Adam said.

"Do you want to?"

"Yeah," I replied. I was confused. There were other people in the room, moving around between the plants. One guy looked up from a tablet he was staring at and gave me a little wave.

"Okay. So as you can see, we grow pot here. We are a respectable business as far as pot growing goes. I mean, we don't cut this stuff with fentanyl or any of that shit. We do hybrids, some oils, sometimes a bit of shatter. But no chemicals. This is about as pure as you can get. Thing is, the government's getting into the game, and the people who buy our stuff will start going to the Weed Board or whatever the hell they're going to call it. So we're looking to *diversify*."

"Not into chemicals," Adam said. "That's what Mike said. No chemicals."

"In fact, the exact opposite. My partner wants to make cider."

"Cider?" I said.

"Like, alcoholic apple juice." Ben rolled his eyes. "I know. But the stuff sells. Thing is, we don't have a lot of capital to start up a new business. I mean, we can get some backers, but we need to show that we're okay sinking our own money into this. Money that we don't have. We have the space, and my partner is getting the equipment. But still, we need money and we need it fast. Faster than these plants can grow. What you see before you is the final batch."

"Mike said something about a club?" Adam said.

"The club. Yeah. It's called Industrial. It's just off King Street. It's been there for ages. But we all know they're only in business to sell drugs. They run their own game in there.

Lots of pills. They have booze as well, but it's the pills people come for. They take five dollars, cash, at the door from anyone who enters. They change the lighting and the music four times a night. And because of that, the clientele changes four times a night. But everyone who comes in pays their five bucks." Ben pulled the cover back over the computer. "This'll get you pissed, Mr. Solo. They say the cover charge is for the DJs, but that's absolute bullshit. The DJs, or at least most of them, do it for free. They think it's building their brand or whatever."

"I don't really DJ anymore," I said quietly.

Ben looked at Adam.

"He can. He's just mostly quit. Nowhere to do it up north."

"Ah, you can still spin though? You have two sets. This Oaklay guy spins hard beats. You cool with that?"

I didn't answer.

"Yeah, he's good," said my brother.

"Maybe I should hear you spin first? You fuck up, and this falls apart. Remember, you're DJ Oaklay. With an *a*."

"He knows," said Adam. "And he's good."

Ben looked at me hard, then shrugged. "All told, we should pull in about fifteen grand."

"No way," I said. I'd never heard of a club having three thousand people show up in one night.

"Likely more," Ben said. "Friday is their big night. As soon as one crowd leaves, another arrives." We followed him back to the kitchen. I caught sight of two guys standing in front of what looked like a giant kettle. They both had beards and dark-framed glasses. Ben shut the door. It felt like the temperature dropped about fifteen degrees.

"What am I doing?" Adam asked.

"You're DJ Oaklay's plus one. You get to go backstage with him, hang out in the green room. Which is right next to the office. And right next to the office is an emergency exit. Tomorrow morning around five a.m., after the chill crowd has settled in, you're going to grab the money and walk out that door."

"What about cameras? Security?"

"They have both for sure."

"So what about Rob?"

"Rob will be gone. He has a five a.m. set, and then he leaves. You linger, grab the cash and meet us outside."

"And why can't you do this yourself?"

"They know us. Plus, we live here. You guys are nobodies. You do this, get in your car and leave town three grand richer."

"Mike said four."

"Did he?" Ben scratched his head. He pulled a large backpack from a hook and shoved it at Adam. "If this bag comes back with more than fifteen in it, you get four. How does that sound?"

"It sounds like something out of my control," Adam said.

"You fill a bag and walk outside. That pays you three grand. It's not complicated."

"No, it's not," Adam agreed.

"This is some Robin Hood shit, man," Ben said, opening the door to the street. There was a bit of a breeze and even though it was pretty hot outside, it still felt cool "We're robbing some bad guys. For a good cause." He smiled a crooked little smile. We stepped outside, and Ben held the door for a moment. "So you're in? You're in one hundred percent?"

"Yeah," Adam said. "We're in."

"You know where the club is?" Adam held his phone up. "Be there at nine. You play at eleven and five. Oh, here." He held a USB stick out to me. "Here's a bunch of the shit this Oaklay guy normally plays. I bet there are full sets on there already mixed. Dude likes to pretend to do stuff, then just wave his arms around. DJ Oaklay with an *a*."

"With an *a*," Adam said, giving Ben a fist bump.

"With an *a*," Ben replied. "We'll see you bright and early tomorrow morning."

He shut the door. Adam immediately walked to the car. I stood there for a few seconds, wondering what the hell had just happened.

Chapter Six

I laid into him the second we got back in the car.

"What the hell is this about? I haven't DJed in almost three years! And you're going to rob these guys? What the hell are you thinking? How is that even possible? Do you think it's all as easy as they make it out to be? The money will just be sitting there in a big bag with a dollar sign on it? Are you out of your mind? And who's Mike? How did you get mixed up in this?"

"Are you done?" my brother asked.

"No, I'm not even close to being done, Adam."

"How about we drive a little and discuss this."

I agreed. I wanted to get the hell away from that house. I was drenched from the heat of that place, and I cranked the AC the second I got the car running.

I pulled onto Queen Street and let Adam direct me. It was rush hour, so the streets were packed with people trying to get home. We moved at a snail's pace, and, with the AC on full blast, I felt my anger begin to subside.

"I know Mike from prison," Adam said. It was the first time I'd heard him use the word. "He did me a favor in there. Ben's his brother. Mike wants to keep him out of trouble, and this cider business seems legit."

"So you're willing to commit a crime to keep someone else out of trouble? Even if it means you could end up back in prison?"

Adam shook his head. "It seems easy enough. Turn right."

I signaled, but no one was letting me in. So I sat there blocking two lanes of traffic. Horns blared.

"You have to be bold, Rob."

I finally caught a break and cut in to head south.

"It's a stupid plan," I said. "There's not a chance it's going to work. I didn't play at that many big clubs, but I'll say this much—they don't just leave money lying around."

"This one does."

"How do you know?"

"I just do. It'll work, Rob, trust me. It has to."

"Why?" We were stuck in more traffic. I put the car into Park. It wasn't even worth trying to move.

"Because I need the money."

"For college?"

"For life. Did you really believe I was serious about going to college?"

"Yes," I said.

"Not a chance. Two more years of sitting around doing nothing? Getting nowhere? If I learned anything from my time…away, it's that you can't waste time. You have to use it or lose it. I don't need to go to school to do what I want to do."

"And what is that?" The traffic started moving again. I put the car into gear and pulled ahead.

"I've got this idea for a T-shirt company."

I shook my head. Everyone had an idea for a T-shirt company. "Really?" I said.

"And other ideas," Adam said defensively. "That's just the start. I'm not going to be broke again, Rob. I'm not going to scrounge any longer. Not having money is the worst thing in this world. You can't do anything. No one gives a shit about you. No one is willing to help you. Anyone with any brains is out there trying to make coin. Without money you're nothing."

We'd made it to King Street. For some reason the traffic started flowing. "Park here real quick," Adam said.

I pulled into a spot but left the car running. The AC washed over us.

"There it is." Adam pointed at the club. Industrial. A small door in a large building. No windows. No top-floor apartments. Just an old warehouse with the name above the door.

"They're going to pull in fifteen grand there tonight?" I said.

"People love this place. I looked it up."

I glanced over at him. He was staring at the building the way a dog stares at a raw piece of meat. "It's a stupid idea," I said.

Adam kept staring. Finally he spoke. "I need you to do this for me, Rob. Okay?"

I didn't reply. Everything inside me told me to say no. To just start driving north and not stop until we got someplace where we could work a full day and get paid for it and make a good living. My brother and I.

The only problem was, I had no idea where that would even be.

"Rob?"

"We can check it out," I said. "That's all I can promise."

"It's going to work," he said. A bus stopped beside us, its air brakes setting off a nearby car alarm. "It has to."

Chapter Seven

There were no turntables. There hadn't been turntables in years. I'd only had them when I was DJing because it was an older club and it had never thrown them out. I liked to actually feel the vinyl. It connected me to the old world of spinning actual records. But the truth was, I didn't need turntables. And I was glad not to be hauling boxes of records with me.

It was all digital. You had any song you wanted in the palm of your hand.

The club was quiet. Adam and I had met with the manager, a guy in his early forties with a giant beard. He'd barely said a word, and the "tour" was basic.

"Green room is over there. DJ booth here," he'd said. Then he'd looked at me. "I thought you'd played here before."

"No."

He'd rubbed at his face. "A lot of these DJ names are the same. Bar's over there. You're of age, right?"

"For sure."

"You're on at eleven and five. No problem there, right?"

"Nope."

"You bring a USB?" I'd held up the stick. "You have half an hour to get yourself familiar with the equipment and plan out a set." And with that he'd walked away.

There was some good music on DJ Oaklay's USB. And some absolute crap. He did have a couple of sets laid out, and I was tempted to just grab one and play it. But that went against everything I'd ever believed in as a DJ. There was an art to mixing music. It wasn't just twisting a knob now and then and bobbing your head.

I began placing tracks next to one another to create a mix. They would still need to be blended together, but I was getting the general idea of how I would spend my hour.

I'd just returned to the first track and was going to practice my fades when Adam stepped up beside me.

"Come back with me for a sec," Adam said.

"Back where?"

"The green room. I need to scope things out."

I was about to tell him to forget it.

But I knew he'd just go on his own. That no matter what I did, Adam was determined to see this through.

The green room was small, sad and musty-smelling. White walls with sagging posters. A sink and microwave. A little fridge.

"Pretty extravagant," Adam said. He shut the door and sat on one of the three couches. The first thing I noticed were the cameras. There were two of them. One facing each door.

"Cameras, eh," I said, opening the fridge. All that was in there was some bottled water and an open container of hummus.

"Yeah. I see that."

"Not making things easy, are they?" I grabbed two bottles of water, handed one to Adam and opened the other.

Adam stood. "Okay. Just wanted to see what we were dealing with here." He hitched up his belt. But his jeans immediately slid back down his thin waist.

Back out in the club, my mix was still playing. It was a combo of the old and the new. I was starting to kind of like DJ Oaklay and wondered what kind of trouble he'd gotten himself into.

The mixing board was tight. None of the dials needed to be turned much for dramatic changes to occur. The bass was heavy and full. The treble high and crisp. Without a doubt this was the best system I'd ever played on.

Adam had brought my headphones, and although I wanted to be angry with him for doing all of this without talking to me first, I also appreciated the comfort and familiarity of my old Sonys.

I didn't know the DJs booked to perform on either side of my slots, so I couldn't build into their work. I decided to create a solid hour of old hard techno. Only one track with lyrics. The rest of the time I'd lay vocals on top of pure drums and bass.

I felt excited to be doing this again. I was really getting into it. Loading the tracks into the mixer. Considering where the drop would be and how to drag it out as long as possible. That was the way I liked to DJ. Make people wait for the drop. Build the set slowly. Get everything to move faster and faster, harder, louder. Then suck the air out of the room with that unbelievable silence before the world came crashing down.

"Nice!" Adam yelled.

I'd decided how to set up the drop. The silence would be killer, followed by an explosion of noise that rumbled out to a heavy hard-techno beat.

"This is a hell of a system!" I yelled. I must have been smiling my face off, because Adam threw an arm around my shoulder and pulled me in tight.

"You still love it," he said.

"I didn't," I replied. "I mean, I quit. This is the first time in, like, three years that I've played." Adam keyed in to what I was saying. "I got into a lot of alt rock stuff."

"What? Like, guitars and shit?"

"Yeah. Deep. I even learned how to play guitar." I shut the music down and ejected the USB stick.

Adam wasn't listening anymore. I looked to where his attention was directed. It seemed as though people were arriving for work. Two large men were sitting at the bar.

"Those'll be the bouncers," said Adam.

"I think we want to stay out of their way," I replied.

"Yeah, you do." A voice behind me made me jump.

Even with the music off, I hadn't heard anyone approach. I spun to find a girl there. She was Asian, her hair was in pigtails, and she had on a panda backpack. She slipped a USB into the console and started flipping switches. "You playing tonight?"

"Yeah," I said.

She held a hand out. "DJ Virtu."

"As in virtuous?"

"No," she said, laughing. "Virtual."

"Oh, okay." I shook her hand. I went to let go, but she held on.

"And you are?"

"DJ Oaklay," I said. "With an *a*."

"Um, no you're not," she said.

"Sorry?" Music suddenly started playing. It had a light, almost fantasy-sounding beat.

"You're not Oaklay. I know him."

"Oh," I said, then didn't know what to say next.

"Oaklay got jammed up and couldn't make it tonight," Adam said. "But if he misses this gig…well, you know. No club likes someone who isn't trustworthy."

"So you're just pretending to be Oaklay?" DJ Virtu asked. I nodded. "You can DJ though, right?"

"Yeah," I said.

"Don't give him a bad name," she said, turning to the console. "He's a friend of mine."

Chapter Eight

We had dinner at a restaurant a block away from the club.

"So," I said, between mouthfuls of pasta. "Do you really think this is going to work?" I was still feeling pretty nervous about it all.

"It's going to work. Trust me," said Adam.

"There are cameras everywhere."

"I don't think the point is that we're going to get away clean and clear with this. I think the point is that no one knows me, and once we've done this I'll be gone. Like, they aren't going to call the cops on me or anything, right?"

"But what if you wanted to come back here?"

Adam wiped at his face with a napkin. "That's in the future. I'm thinking about right now."

This was Adam all over. He'd only ever thought about "right now." The future had always been something he couldn't even imagine.

"It's stealing," I said quietly.

"I know it is. But they've been ripping DJs off forever. They tell everyone that the DJs get the door, but they don't. It's full-on Robin Hood, Rob."

"I'm not sure they'll see it that way," I said.

"I'm not really worried about what way they'll see it. I need to get paid."

I didn't like it, but I finished my pasta and tried to imagine it all working out like he said it would. I knew I couldn't stop him. But maybe, somehow, I could save him.

We got to the club early. It didn't open until ten. We were banging on the door at nine thirty.

"Eager," one of the giant bouncers said as he let us in. We were almost past him when he said, "Have I seen you guys here before?"

"No," I said. "We're from New York." I don't know what made me say that. I guess it seemed possible, and to be from a place far away from Toronto made sense.

"I expect to hear some solid NY beats then," the bouncer said. He held out his hand, and we went through an elaborate shake that I always seemed to be a step behind with. DJ Virtu was already in the booth. The system was humming, but nothing was playing yet.

"You came back," Virtu said as I stepped inside and Adam went to the bar and settled himself onto a stool. "I wasn't sure you would."

"Why not?" I replied.

Virtu hit a button, and a steady, slow, heaving beat filled the room. Everything changed then, as it always does with the introduction of music to a silent room. "No reason!" she yelled. I stared at her, and she added, "You just looked like you might be in over your head."

The doors of the club opened, and a few people came in. I could see them handing over five-dollar bills. Virtu dropped a vocal line over the beats. I watched as she set the lights to pulse. She mixed one track into the next, and had I not watched her do it, I wouldn't have known it had happened. She was very smooth.

After she had the next track rolling, she turned to me, looking a little surprised. "You're still here?"

"Oh, sorry."

She shifted toward me and spread her arms wide. "Yeah, I need my space."

I stepped out of the booth and went to the bar.

"This place is filling up fast," Adam said. He'd spun around on the stool to take in the ever-growing crowd. "I don't think they were shitting us about the three thousand."

We sat there just watching right up until I needed to get into the booth. There were at least five hundred people in the giant space by then. Eleven o'clock was pretty early for a club crowd. I was growing more convinced that there could very well be three thousand people coming through the door that night.

"I gotta spin," I said. Adam gave me a clap on the back.

DJ Virtu spotted me as I climbed the steps to the booth.

"Do you want me to end or let it ride?"

"Let it ride!" I yelled. It was etiquette. If you had the preceding DJ shut their track down, you were pretty much saying you didn't like their music and didn't want to be associated with what they were spinning. If you let it ride, it meant you wanted to work with them. To blend your sets together because you approved of their set.

"I'll leave you something interesting." She turned back to the console, and the beat suddenly pitched up. It sounded almost like a jungle track with its skipping, jumping beats. She hit the lights a few times, then raised her arms and screamed into the microphone, "DJ Virtu out. I'll be back at four. See you all then!"

People clapped and yelled. She leaned back over the microphone. "DJ Oaklay, people!"

I shrunk. It wasn't my name. But it was still me standing up there. As she passed me, Virtu said, "Do him proud."

"I'll try."

I inserted the USB and found the directory I'd set up before. The songs I wanted to use were all there. I had planned out the order. But suddenly I was fumbling with the dials. I couldn't get the first track started properly. I kept missing the timing as the crazy song Virtu had put on seemed to be constantly speeding up. I closed my eyes and breathed for a moment. Let the music swell around me. Then I tried again.

Everything slowed down. And it was just like in the old days. I could slip into the beat wherever I wanted. Play with it. Blend the next track in as though the two had been made together. When I got the first track mixed, I looked up to see a room filled with people dancing. Adam was right there at the front, waving his arms and nodding to the beat. I played with the bass a little, making the speakers *whomp*. I held the treble a touch higher than it needed to be, then mixed in the next track, which had no real treble at all. It was like a mini drop. All that high end and then nothing but bass.

The time slipped away. The room filled. The tracks seemed to mix themselves. I felt like the guy I had once been. The guy who loved this. Who wanted to control a crowd. To give these people what they demanded. To make music *from* music. None of it was mine, but in the end I created something new from it.

I looked up at one point, and there was a skinny dude wearing all black standing there.

"End it right at midnight," he said. "I like a clean slate."

"Sounds good to me," I yelled back. I'd been building the beat toward a drop. I could tell the crowd was feeling it. I checked the time. Inched the speed up one last step and then, when the music was no longer music, no longer sound but more of a force of nature throbbing in the empty spaces of the club, I cut to silence.

It was as if all the air had been sucked from the room. Then I dropped a high-end track. All fast beats and dizzying whistles and bells. I pulled the USB from the console and nodded to the other DJ.

"You can play with that or let it end," I said.

The crowd was going insane. The DJ looked at them, inserted his USB and said, "Yeah, man, I think I'll keep this going."

Chapter Nine

We spent the next three hours being pummeled by heavy, happy beats. I got so into the music, into the technicality of what was going on in the DJ booth, that I forgot why we were truly there. Adam would drag me into the green room every half hour or so. He'd open the fridge, look around and then go back out to the bar.

"Do you think those cameras actually record? Or is it a live feed that someone monitors all the time?" Adam asked.

"I imagine they record," I replied. Maybe that would make Adam rethink his plan. It was four forty-five. I was about to go on again. "We don't have to do this. I could get back into DJing. You could manage me, take a cut, take it all, whatever. We really don't have to do this."

"What about school? And anyway, you wouldn't make much DJing," he said. "Not enough. We need capital."

"I don't know," I said. "If someone's monitoring that feed, they'll be on you right away. If they aren't, they're going to find out who you are and hunt you down." I was thinking of myself as well. Thinking about how DJ Virtu knew I wasn't Oaklay. There were so many ways that this might not turn out well for us. We could be caught immediately, and if not now, then later. They were not just going to let go of fifteen thousand dollars.

I was exhausted. It had been an incredibly long day and night, and I'd spent too much of it trying to figure out a way to stop Adam from doing what he was about to do. I could tell he was prepared though. His eyes were wide open and wild. He kept jiggling his leg.

"The bouncers stay at the door," Adam said. "One of them went to the back once, but that's been it. I haven't seen anyone inside the office, not in all the times we've been in the green room."

"The cameras—"

"I don't care about the cameras. I just care about getting the money and getting out the door. After that we're free."

"You really don't think they're going to try to find you someday?"

"I don't doubt they will," he said. "But I don't care. I'm going to be gone."

"You mean you want to stay up north forever?"

"I don't want to stay up north for even a minute." He was staring at the mass of people dancing in front of us. When I wasn't in the DJ booth, it always seemed like madness on the dance floor. People swinging, waving their arms, shaking their heads to the beat. I knew people for whom this was their entire life. They just spent hours shaking their arms and dancing, and for the rest of the week all they thought about was doing it again.

"You mean you're leaving again?"

"The last time I left, it wasn't my choice," Adam said. He took a swig from whatever he'd been drinking. "This time it will be."

"You're just going to leave us again?" I repeated.

"You can come with me."

"What kind of plan is that?" I asked. "Where do you think you can go on three thousand dollars?"

"It's a start, Rob," he said. "I have to be somewhere else."

"So that's how you're going to spend the rest of your life? Running from place to place whenever things get too difficult?" I think my anger surprised him. But then, he didn't know everything I had been through. How could he?

"What are you getting all bent out of shape for, Rob?"

"It was your stupidity that got you into jail last time," I said. "Trying to be the man or whatever was going on there. Do you know how hard it was on Mom, having a son in jail? Never knowing what was going to happen to him?" Adam looked away, but I wasn't going to let him off the hook. "And me. I had a brother, and then I didn't."

"I'm still here," Adam said weakly.

"But you weren't. And now you're going to leave again." We had to yell our conversation over the beats. A couple of guys who had been sitting near us had left. We were virtually alone in a little corner of the bar. The crowd was cheering for the DJ.

"If I learned one thing in prison, Rob," Adam said, "it's that you have to be your own man. You have to think for yourself. And you have to do what is right for you."

"That's great. Forget about your family, your friends—just look out for number one. Great lesson." I was pissed, but I also understood that there was no way I was going to change Adam's mind. He was going to do this. I checked my phone. My set would start soon.

"I'm not supposed to go back there until just before six," Adam said. "They shut the doors at six thirty and then the bouncer takes the last of the money back to the office. There should be piles of it."

"I don't care what you're going to do," I said.

"This doesn't have anything to do with you, Rob!" Adam yelled.

"It has everything to do with me, Adam. But you go ahead and just think about yourself." I stood and took one step toward the booth. He grabbed my arm. He looked me in the eye. I remembered all the times that he had been there for me. Beating up bullies at school, talking me through things when Dad left, answering my never-ending questions. Just being there. And now here he was, deciding *again* not to be there.

"Don't screw this up for me, Rob," he said.

I shook off his arm and stormed up to the booth.

Chapter Ten

Nobody wants hard, heavy beats at five o'clock in the morning. Or, at least, those who do are generally not welcome in a club at that time. Mine was the first "chill" set. Music designed to slow everyone down. To ease into morning. The thing with people who enjoy this kind of music, these kinds of clubs, is that they hold on to their desires for an entire week before letting loose for one night. So they make the most of it.

I wasn't surprised to see the crowd thinning slightly and then, as I stepped into the DJ booth, begin to grow again. Most clubs close around four a.m. But the odd club, like this one, runs until daylight and beyond.

I started out with one of my favorite old chill tunes from Orbital. I could have let that dreamy track play for its full ten minutes. I figured everyone in the crowd would have been absolutely fine with it. Instead, after two minutes I began looping other tracks over it. I fed songs in and out of the mix, moving the jittery beat forward and back until it began to sound as though every song was this one song. It was a trick I'd picked up years before, and it took me as close as I could ever get to actually making my own music.

The DJ booth sat high in one corner of the club, giving an incredible view of the crowd. I kept the lights flashing in subdued tones but bright enough that the entire club floor was lit every few seconds. The dancers looked as though they were jumping through time, their movements quick yet blurred.

As I was turning up the treble, I noticed more people coming in the door. A group of girls, a couple of guys who looked as though they'd had a very, very long night already, then Ben. He was with two other guys. I couldn't be certain, but they looked like the guys I'd seen in the grow op.

I thought I remembered Ben saying he couldn't be seen in this club. But there he was, shaking hands with the bouncer. Then, very quickly, the four of them moved along the wall, behind the bar and through the door near the green room.

I leaned over the console, looking for Adam. Hoping he'd just seen what I had. He was close to the booth, lazily drifting back and forth. There was no way he would have seen Ben and the other guys come in. Not from where he was. Unless you were at the front door or where I was, up high in the booth, it would have been impossible to see them enter.

I kept mixing, trying to figure out what I should do. Why were they here?

Ben exited the back room first. He was carrying a full-looking backpack. The other two guys followed, carrying backpacks too. They all hurried out the door, and the bouncer held it open for them. Only one of the bouncers was at the door. I scanned the room, looking for the other one. I spotted him lounging on a couch, surrounded by a small group of people. He was laughing and talking animatedly. I watched as he pulled his phone from his pocket, looked at it and stood up. He returned to the door.

In a flash, it all began to make sense to me. The way Ben had been so quick to set us up with this "opportunity." The way he had rushed us from the grow op. He had told us they wanted to start a different business. That this was all Robin Hood stuff. Stealing from the rich, giving to the poor. He'd made all the right sounds, but his actions weren't adding up.

I mixed a track that would run to the end of my time and, thankfully, found the next DJ mounting the stairs. "Want that to run out?" I asked. "Or stop it?"

The guy barely looked at me. "I'll deal with it." He held a fist out, and I gave it a bump. "That was a sweet set. Very chill."

"Thanks." I darted down the stairs, looking in both directions for Adam. He wasn't where he'd been. Nor was he at the bar. I spun around, trying to locate him. Then I zeroed in on the door to the green room just in time to watch it closing behind my brother.

Chapter Eleven

Adam was in front of the little fridge when I ran in.

"It's a setup, Adam," I said.

He turned and looked at me. He seemed confused. "Shut up, Rob."

"I just saw Ben and those two other guys from the grow up leave the club with full backpacks."

"So what?"

"Ben said they couldn't come in here. That they were banned or something. Which was why we had to do this. But they were just here with one of the bouncers."

Adam moved to the door that separated the green room from the office. The backpack he'd been given, almost identical to the ones I had just watched Ben and his friends leave with, was slung over his shoulders.

It struck me that if there actually *was* fifteen thousand dollars in five-dollar bills, a single backpack couldn't possibly hold it all. All three of those other guys had been carrying backpacks, and they'd all looked very, very full.

"It's not a setup," he said. "I just watched the bouncer come in here with a lockbox."

"I don't know *how* it's a setup, but it is. I swear to you it is. How would you even fit fifteen thousand dollars in there?" I said, pointing at the backpack.

"There'll be other bags in there. How else would they get it all out?"

"Think about fifteen thousand dollars, Adam. Even in hundreds, it wouldn't fit in three of those bags." I thought of the last guy leaving the club, two backpacks on him. One slung over each shoulder.

"Rob, I need this capital. There's a lot you're not getting here." He closed his eyes and then opened them again. "Aren't you still supposed to be DJing?"

"I'm done," I said.

"You're screwing everything up. Just go. Go out the front. Wait for me at the car."

"No," I said. "It's a setup, Adam."

"Saying it over and over again doesn't make it any more true."

"I know it is." My throat got itchy and raw. I was suddenly sniffling. I pulled my sleeve across my eyes. "You're going to end up back in prison."

"I'm not. You're wrong. I'm getting out of here."

I took a step toward him. "I forgive you for what happened," I said.

Adam froze.

"All the time we lost together. All the times I really needed a brother. But if you do this, I won't forgive you again. You're being set up. And even if you aren't, it's not right. It's not the way to turn things around."

He stood there staring at me. His hand on the door handle.

"I swear, Adam, you'll be dead to me if you go in there."

He kept staring. I had no idea what was going through his head right then. What he was contemplating. But after a few seconds he let go of the handle.

"We'll talk to Ben," he said. "Tell him this was just to scope things out. We can do it next week."

"We're not doing it," I said.

"If it's a setup, Rob, then we'll know. Right? We'll know right away. Then we can talk about it."

It was all he had to offer, so I had to take it. "Let's get out of here," I said.

As we turned, DJ Virtu came through the door. She seemed surprised to see us standing there. "What are you two still doing back here?" she asked.

Adam held up the water bottle. "Grabbing a drink before we go," he said.

DJ Virtu tilted her head to one side. I could see she was looking at the door to the office. "Anyone in there?" she asked.

"I don't know," I replied. "Isn't it, like, a storage space or something?"

"It's the office," she said, crossing the room. As she reached for the door handle, Adam and I left the green room. "Where are you two going?" she called.

"My set is done," I called back. "We're out of here."

"What were you doing in here?" DJ Virtu asked. "Rob, what were you doing in here?"

I froze at the sound of my name. I hadn't told her my name. All I'd said was that I was pretending to be DJ Oaklay. Nothing else.

"How do you know my name?" I asked. Adam was a couple steps ahead of me. He stopped.

"You told me," she said.

"No I didn't." And even though I wasn't certain of much at this moment, I was sure of that. I remembered the conversation perfectly. "I never told you my name."

She slammed the door shut and followed us out of the green room. "You were doing something in the office," she said. "I know you were."

"I thought that was a storage room," I said. "Like I told you."

She scrunched up her face and grabbed my arm.

"I know you were doing something. You were—"

But she never got the chance to finish because the room suddenly filled with light and the music ground to a halt.

Chapter Twelve

"Sorry, everyone. This is Jared, the manager here." Everyone looked toward the DJ booth, where the manager was speaking into the microphone. "There have been some difficulties, and we're going to have to close early. Please move to the exit doors in as orderly a fashion as possible." He must have realized he sounded too official because he followed this up with, "Feels like a school fire drill, doesn't it? Our bouncers will give you a card on your way out. You can use it for one free entry at any time." This seemed to get people moving.

DJ Virtu let go of my arm and stepped back into the green room. Adam and I joined the line of people heading toward the door. I watched as the bouncer handed out cards. He kept looking up, scanning the people coming toward him.

"What do you think this is about?" Adam asked.

"I don't even have to guess," I replied. It was all clicking into place. We were being played. I figured Ben, or whatever his name was, had asked his buddy in jail for the name of someone who was going to be released soon. Someone he could easily hang a theft like this on. Then he'd made a deal with the bouncer and the other two guys. Which meant they would have left some of the money in the office. Not much, but it would look like a lot. Adam wasn't dumb, but he would have grabbed whatever he could when he got in there, that much I knew. Which would have been exactly what those guys were expecting. I bet there wasn't even a DJ Oaklay who suddenly couldn't play that night.

Which meant DJ Virtu had been in on it as well.

"Why do you have a pack?" the bouncer asked as we stepped up in front of him.

"He brought some records," Adam said, pointing at me.

"Where are the records now?"

"Up in the booth," I said. "I didn't know there weren't real turntables here."

"What's in the pack?" The bouncer I'd seen go into the office with Ben and his buddies was suddenly beside us. He grabbed the pack and ripped it open.

"Like I was just saying," Adam said, "there were records in it. Now it's empty."

"Records?" the bouncer said. He looked baffled. The line had come to a complete halt.

Jared was suddenly behind us. "What's the holdup?"

"This guy has a backpack," the bouncer said. His face had gone white, his eyes wide.

"And what's in it?" Jared asked.

Adam took his pack back from the bouncer. "Nothing. Like I just told your bouncer, it had records in it. But you don't have real turntables here."

Jared laughed. "Who uses real turntables anymore?"

"I guess no one," Adam said. He zipped up the pack.

Jared looked at the bouncers. "Find anything yet?"

The bouncers shook their heads.

"Keep looking."

The bouncers separated so we could get past, and a moment later we were out on the street.

It's always strange coming out of a dark club and into daylight. The light seems that much more bright. The breeze that much cooler. The street noise dulled.

We walked to the car and got in. Adam sat for a while, staring straight ahead. We could see the club from where we were. People were exiting and being shocked by the brightness of daylight. It was almost comical.

I didn't say anything to Adam. I just let him sit there and think. Then I noticed something I hadn't before. Something we really should have seen earlier, but in our hurry to get inside just didn't see.

"Look at the side of the building," I said.

Adam shook his head as if to clear it and then looked to where I was pointing. "Yeah, what about it?"

"Notice anything?"

"Like what?" The alley had garbage bins, a couple of old bikes and some exhaust pipes for air conditioning. But something was missing.

"No exit doors," I said.

Adam looked closer. "Holy shit."

"It was a setup," I said, but with absolutely no satisfaction.

"It was," Adam replied. He started the car, but before he put it into Drive he glanced at me. "Thanks," he said.

"Yeah," I said. "Someone has to look after you."

Chapter Thirteen

We stopped at the college on the way
out of town. There weren't many people
around, but we found all the program
information we needed.

"It's actually pretty cool here,"
Adam said. We wandered the campus
before going into a café to get some
coffee and something to eat. We sat
outside and watched people walk past.

Adam flipped through the program information.

"What do you see me as?" he asked. "An electrician? A graphic designer? A hairdresser?"

"Did you pick up that last one by mistake?"

"Yeah, maybe."

"Graphic design," I said.

"I might do electrician. It says they offer apprenticeships. I could do that for a while and then start to think about graphic design."

"Probably a good idea," I said. I looked at the brochure for the electrician program. It seemed like it would be interesting. And totally something I could see Adam doing. But it didn't matter to me what he was doing as long as he was in school and not trying to figure out a new way to get rich quick.

I was incredibly tired, and my stomach clenched against the coffee.

"I have to hit the washroom," I said, standing. Adam was still looking at the brochures. He nodded.

The quiet and peace of the single-stall washroom was such a relief that I spent more time in there than I needed to. I threw water on my face and dried it off a couple of times. We had been so close to disaster. So close I didn't even want to think about it.

When I got back to the table, Adam was staring into his coffee.

"You okay?" I asked as I sat down.

"That was stupid," he said. "So stupid. Why am I so stupid?"

"You're not," I said.

"Prove it."

"You're sitting here, not going back to jail."

"That's only because of you."

"You made your own choice back there. You decided not to do it."

He nodded but didn't seem convinced.

"It was close," I said.

"Really close. I never should have trusted Mike. He was always dodgy." He looked up at me, his eyes bright and glistening. "I guess I wanted to believe it could be that easy."

"I know," I said.

"Maybe I should stop looking for the easy way." I didn't reply. "You have no idea what it's like in prison."

"I don't."

"You have to get hard to survive. You have to look for ways to get ahead. Just little things. An extra shift in the library or kitchen to have something to do. The right friends so you don't always have to be looking over your shoulder. It's so tiring, Rob."

"Yeah," I said.

"I don't want to do it again." He'd started to cry. I hadn't even noticed it. I heard it in his voice, and then he was wiping at his eyes. "Ever."

"You won't," I said. "Get into this program. Get the apprenticeship or whatever, and it's like none of this ever happened."

"It'll never be like none of this ever happened," Adam said.

"It could be close," I said.

"Yeah. I guess it could."

We talked more on the ride home, but not about what was going to happen next. Instead it was about other car rides we'd taken. About the cottage we used to visit. The days that seemed so far in our past that they might as well have belonged to other people. But they didn't. They were ours.

Eventually I fell asleep, and I didn't wake up until we were just on the edge of our town. I sat up with a horrible taste in my mouth.

"What time is it?"

"Late afternoon," Adam said, laughing. "It's been a day."

"I can't wait to go to bed."

"Dude, you just slept for, like, three hours. I'm the one who can't wait to go to bed."

We pulled up outside the house. The front door was open. Mom was out on the porch with a cup of coffee in her hands. She waved to us.

"Don't tell her what happened," Adam said.

"There's no way I would say a word to her."

Adam grabbed the brochures. "I don't want to disappoint her anymore."

"I think you're heading in the right direction," I said.

He nodded to this, then opened his door and stepped outside.

"How was it?" Mom asked.

Adam got hyped up, waving the brochures as he crossed the lawn.

"Electrician," Adam said.

Mom's face lit up. It was really good to see.

"Yeah?"

"Everyone needs electricity, right?"

We sat down on either side of Mom, and Adam began describing the school. The buildings and people and how he felt so energized there. He went quiet for a moment, and Mom laid her head on his shoulder.

"This is going to be good," she said.

"It is," Adam replied. "I know it is."

Chapter Fourteen

Adam went to college that fall. He took some online courses over the summer to upgrade his math and English, and by September he was ready for the full-time program. Mom and I moved to a little place called Ancaster, just outside Hamilton. Close enough to Adam that we could see him now and then, but far enough away that it didn't seem like we were following him.

Which we totally were.

One weekend he came to see us and we all went for ice cream at this place in the little downtown core. We sat outside, even though it was a cool evening. We'd been sitting there for half an hour in near silence when a memory surfaced. But it didn't feel like a memory. It felt like a dream that had come to life. Or something we'd done long ago and completely forgotten about.

"Do you guys believe in déjà vu?" I asked.

Mom looked at me and considered this.

"I've had it happen," she said. "Like when you stop and go, *Wait, didn't this already happen*?"

"Exactly," I said.

"Maybe we've had some moment in our minds that we hope will happen one day, and when it does we remember that desire."

"Maybe," I said. It was so strong a feeling, though, that I could taste it. The ice cream. The sun setting. The cool air pushing into the folds of my hoodie.

"I think it's something different," Adam said. "I think it's, like, a message that you're in the right spot."

"How so?"

"I don't know. I just know that whenever it has happened to me, good things were happening. Or were about to."

Adam licked his ice cream, and it was there again. That feeling I'd seen all of this before.

And then I remembered.

We'd been at the cottage. It was on a little lake, and Adam and I had been given some money to go buy ice cream. Instead of walking, though, we'd taken a canoe. The ice-cream stand was on the other side of the lake, but instead of paddling straight across, we'd gone along the shore the whole way around. It had taken hours, or at least it had felt that way at the time. We'd seen fish and geese, and people had waved to us as if we were some kind of royalty. But when we got to the ice-cream place, it was closed. We felt horrible. We'd spent so long getting there, and we were tired out. We had sat down in front of the place and just stared at the water. Talked about how much it sucked. Adam had looked at the stand a bunch of times. He'd seemed really angry. Then he'd gotten up, walked over to it and just stood there staring at it.

Then, out of nowhere, a teenage girl had come walking around the side of the stand.

"Were you two wanting ice cream?" she asked.

"Yeah!" Adam and I both said.

"I saw you from my house. I closed early to look after my brother, but my parents are home now."

She'd opened the stand and gone inside.

I remembered the whirring of the motor for the fridge. The clack of the big window opening. And all the kinds of ice cream laid out before us.

"You can have two scoops for the price of one for being so patient," she said. I'd picked chocolate and mint. Adam went with strawberry and vanilla.

We'd thanked the girl and she'd shut the whole thing down again and left.

Then we'd sat at the picnic table out front and eaten the cones in silence. Side by side at the picnic table, looking out over this lake at dusk.

My brother and me.

"I think you're right," I said, watching Adam pop the end of his cone into his mouth. "You get déjà vu when something good is about to happen."

He smiled at me, and that was what I remembered. The smile that said he was thinking, wondering, considering, always ready for the next big thing. For now, he looked content.

Jeff Ross is the author of several novels for young adults, including the Orca Soundings titles *Coming Clean* and *Up North* also featuring Rob Maclean and his brother Adam. He teaches script-writing and English at Algonquin College in Ottawa.

DON'T MISS OUT ON MORE ROB AND ADAM MACLEAN!

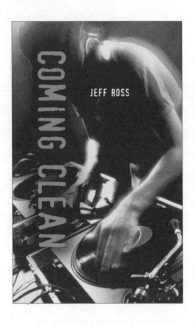

Rob wants to be a DJ, but when a girl overdoses during his first gig and his brother is implicated, Rob realizes he could lose everything.

"Powerfully sharp."—*Booklist*

"A quick paced story, compelling and real… Highly Recommended."—*CM Magazine*

Racial tensions run high in a small northern town, and after Rob witnesses a violent incident, the police are pressuring him to identify their prime suspect.

"A very good novel that leaves readers thinking about their own views…Recommended."
—*CM Magazine*

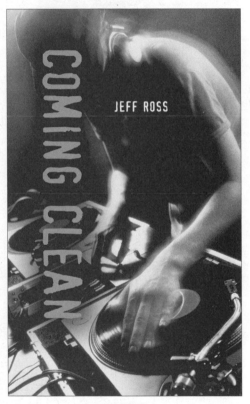

JEFF ROSS

COMING CLEAN

9781459803312 PB

Chapter One

The problem with my brother is that he is far too often full of it. Which is why I was skeptical when he said he'd landed me a DJ gig at the local all-ages club.

"Friday night," he said.

"Seriously, Adam, don't mess with me right now." I was in my room trying to beat match an old soul record with a white label drum and bass LP. It was not going well.

"I'm serious, Rob. I got you this Friday night!"

"Adam," I said, taking my headphones off and silencing the stereo. "DJ Sly does Friday nights at The Disco." DJ Sly was a ridiculous name for a DJ. The Disco was a ridiculous name for an all-ages club. And yet, at that time I would have done anything to be DJ Sly playing at The Disco. Proving yet again that life, at its core, is a cruel joke.

"Do you mean the DJ Sly who just recently took a nasty tumble and busted his wrist? That DJ Sly?"

"What?" I said. "I never heard about that."

"That's because it happened yesterday and you, as far as I can tell, have been locked in here for the past week." He looked at the floor where there were piles of dirty plates and glasses. Mom had been working double shifts, leaving the two of us to our own devices.

Always a bad idea.

Adam is taller than me by about three inches. He's also thicker. I've never been able to break 120 pounds while Adam is a steady 160. He is far too fond of hair gel. His black curls are totally glued to his head. I have longer hair and let it do what it wants. And yet there's always talk about how we look so much alike. Adam has small eyes, which some people might refer to as beady. And his nose is a little too big for the rest of his face. It's these kinds of characteristics that people seem to become depressed about. Like, there's nothing you can do about the size of your eyes or nose, but people are going to make you feel bad about it anyway. Adam also had some pretty severe acne for a while, and his constant action against the angry red balls has left his skin pock-marked and rutted.

In the end, though, neither of us are hideous. But Adam has cared too much for too long about how he looks, and now he often walks hunched over with a hoodie pulled up around his face. Though I have noticed that in the past few months he's begun to stand a little straighter.

"Anyway, Sly is down for the count and he needs a replacement."

"And how did you get me Sly's night?" I dropped my headphones around my neck. I then cleared a bunch of records off my bed to make room to sit down.

"I've been working there. You know that." Adam leaned against the door frame and examined a fingernail.

"So you've been saying. What, exactly, is your job?"

"This and that. What does it matter? I got you the night, Rob. You can do this, right? I haven't just made myself look like an ass on your account, have I?"

I looked at my crates of LPS. A lot of DJs had moved onto digital MP3 turntables. But MP3s sound awful, in my opinion. When you put a poorly encoded song through a giant system like they have at The Disco, it sounds like you're listening to music underwater. Everything is floppy and round sounding. Records are crisp. The beats hard.

Besides, I can't afford a laptop to run it all.

"For sure," I said, sounding as confident as possible.

"It's a big night, man," Adam said. He hadn't moved from the doorway. I knew exactly why. He wanted to be thanked for his awesomeness."

"Yeah, it'll be huge. Thanks, man."

"No problem." He swiveled off the door frame and put his fist out in front of him. I gave it a quick pump.

"How long is my set?"

"Three hours. You go on at nine. DJ Lookie takes over at midnight."

"Awesome," I said, getting excited about it. "Thanks, man. Seriously."

orca soundings

For more information on all the books
in the Orca Soundings series, please visit
orcabook.com.